Contents

Ladybird books are widely available, but in case of
difficulty may be ordered by post or telephone from:

Ladybird Books – Cash Sales Department
Littlegate Road Paignton Devon TQ3 3BE
Telephone 0803 554761

A catalogue record for this book is available
from the British Library

Published by Ladybird Books Ltd Loughborough Leicestershire UK
Ladybird Books Inc Auburn Maine 04210 USA

Text © JOAN STIMSON 1994
Illustrations © NIGEL McMULLEN 1994
LADYBIRD and the device of a Ladybird are trademarks of Ladybird Books Ltd

Two Minute
Minute
Teddy Bear
Tales

by Joan Stimson

illustrated by Nigel McMullen

The Bear at the Bus Stop

"Look Dad," cried the girl, "someone's left their teddy at the bus stop."

"So they have," said Dad. "Do you think we should take him home with us?"

"Oh no!" cried the girl. "His owner will be back soon and Teddy wouldn't be here for him."

Just then the bus came. And the girl and her Dad disappeared.

Before the next bus,
a lady came along.
She was on her way
to a Jumble Sale.

"WOULDN'T you look
nice on my Book and Toy
Stall!" she told Teddy.

But then the lady thought again.

"I'm sure your owner will be here very
soon. So here's one of my books to sit on.
And now you can see out while you wait."

Before the next bus, a childminder arrived. Her children squealed and pointed. "I want that bear," they all cried together.

But the childminder was firm. "That bear belongs to someone else," she said. "But I'm sure he won't mind if we read his book while we wait."

The children enjoyed Teddy's book so much that they left him one of their chewy bars.

Before the next bus,
three big boys
came along.

"Hey!" they cried.
"It's a bear we can
chuck around on the
bus." And the biggest boy
made a grab for Teddy.

WHOOPS! Off came Teddy's arm.

"How was I to know his arm was loose?"
complained the biggest boy. And he delved
in his pocket for his *wonder knife.*

Carefully and very gently the biggest boy
put Teddy back together. "Better than he
was in the first place!" he beamed.

All day long the people who had met Teddy wondered if he would be all right. When they got off the bus that night, they couldn't wait to see if he was still there.

"Oh!" they all said in turn. "He's gone!"

But then they spotted a note:

Dear Passengers,
Thank you for my lovely book and chewy bar. Thank you for mending my arm. (It's much more comfortable now.) But, most of all, thank you for leaving me at the bus stop... for my owner.
Love,
Teddy X

Another
story
tomorrow.

It Was Teddy!

Carl was a careless small boy. But he didn't like to admit it.

So, when he turned on the taps and flooded the bathroom, he wouldn't own up. "It was Teddy!" he told his parents.

The same thing happened when Carl took an ice cream from the fridge, and left it to melt.

"What a waste!" said Mum.

"What a CARELESS Teddy!" sighed Carl.

And then one day Carl accidentally hurled a ball through Mrs Weaver's window.

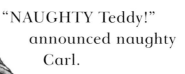

"NAUGHTY Teddy!" announced naughty Carl.

"Teddy is beginning to get expensive," said Dad. And he decided to talk to Carl's teacher.

Now Carl and Teddy were still new boys.
But Carl enjoyed school and he worked
hard.

"Next week," Miss Mulberry told the
children, "we are having an important
visitor. And I want you all to make her
a nice picture."

Carl painted his best picture ever.
Miss Mulberry put it on the wall along
with the others.

When the important visitor arrived, she was impressed. "What wonderful paintings!" she exclaimed. Then she took a closer look and pointed to Carl's. "Whoever painted this one?" she asked. "It's outstanding."

Carl squirmed with pride and Miss Mulberry smiled across the room. "It was Teddy!" she told the visitor.

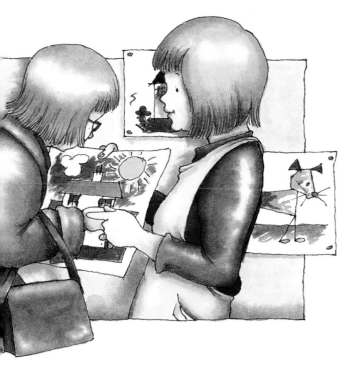

That evening Carl took a glass of milk up to his bedroom. But he soon came down again.

"Sorry Dad," said Carl, "I've spilt my milk and made a mess."

Mum looked amazed. "Whoever taught you to own up?" she asked.

Carl beamed at his parents. Then he told them, "IT WAS TEDDY!"

16

Another story tomorrow.

17

The Bear Who Didn't Like Hugs

"Excuse me!" muttered Panda. And he shuffled to the back of the window display.

"What ARE you doing?" grumbled the other bears.

"Don't you WANT to be sold?" growled Large Brown. And he slid smartly into Panda's space.

Just at that moment a tiny girl bounced along the pavement. She pointed at Large Brown and dragged her mum inside.

The shopkeeper reached carefully into the display. He scooped up Large Brown and presented him to the girl.

"OOOOOOH!" she squealed. And gave him a huge hug.

"Hooray!" whispered the other bears... all except Panda.

"Whatever's the matter?" squeaked Plump Blue. "Don't you want to go to a good home?"

Panda shook his head. "I don't like hugs!" he mumbled.

"Why ever not?" asked the other bears. "You'll NEVER find a kind owner, if you don't!"

Weeks passed and bears came and went.

'I wish *I* could be sold!" sighed Plump Blue.

"I don't!" muttered Panda, and he settled down to snooze.

Suddenly he was woken by an excited shriek. It was a plump girl in a blue track suit. And she was pointing straight at Panda.

"Come on, Grandad," she cried. "Let's go into the shop."

Panda held his breath. The shopkeeper reached briskly into the display. SCOOP! "Here's Panda," he said. But then he scooped again. "And here's a VERY cuddly teddy." The shopkeeper presented the girl with Plump Blue.

Somehow they seemed made for each other. The girl couldn't stop hugging Plump Blue. And Panda heaved a sigh of relief. But Panda was in for a shock.

"We'll take BOTH bears!" Grandad told the shopkeeper.

When they reached the girl's home, her mum scolded Grandad. "Fancy buying TWO teddies," she exclaimed.

"HRUMPH!" Grandad looked sheepish. Then he explained. "The Panda's for me," he said. "He reminds me of my very first bear. And he looks just the sort of chap to keep me company... in my long-distance lorry."

Panda couldn't believe his ears. He couldn't wait to become a long-distance bear. And, although he never DID get to like hugs, when Grandad patted his shoulder each night and said, "Home at last," Panda was the happiest bear on the road.

Another story tomorrow.

Seven Sporty Bears

Monday's bear runs far and wide,
Tuesday's bear can bike and ride;

Wednesday's bear plays pool with me,
Thursday's bear can climb a tree;

Friday's bear WILL jump in puddles,
Saturday's bear is best at cuddles;

But Sunday's bear, I'm proud to say,
Has just scored a goal...
Hip, hip, HOORAY!

Turn over for another teddy bear rhyme.

25

Midnight in the Park

You know the bear from Number Nine,
She likes to play at night;
DOWN the drainpipe watch her whizz,
There's not a soul in sight.

She tries a cartwheel on the grass,
She longs to stretch her paws,
Then on the swing she starts to sing,
"It's great to be outdoors!"

"Psst!" Someone's creeping up the path,
They want to try the slide,
It's Twenty three and Seven B,
"We couldn't stay inside."

Now Twenty two is coming too,
And Seventeen and Four,
They're jumping off the
  climbing frame,
Then running back for more.

But suddenly a light appears,
"What's going on out there?"
A small boy cries and tries to see,
"And where's my teddy bear?"

UP the drainpipe home they go
Before it starts to rain,
They leave the park all still
  and dark,
But they'll be back again!

Turn
over for
another teddy
bear rhyme.

Hand Wash with Care

A bear likes to snack,
A bear likes to share,
So, if there's chocolate on his nose...
Hand wash with care.

A bear likes to bake
Cakes beyond compare,
So, if there's jam between his toes...
Hand wash with care.

A bear likes to paint,
He has artistic flair,
So, if there's green behind his ears...
Hand wash with care.

A bear likes to play
And accidents are rare,
But, if a muddy paw appears...
Hand wash with care.

A bear likes to... EXPLORE
And that's his own affair,
You'll catch him looking rather red
While peeking here and there!

And, if disaster strikes,
We think it's only fair,
To wash his clothes while he's in bed...
MACHINE wash with care.

Another story tomorrow.

A Stitch in Time

"Cheer up, Teddy!"
began Rabbit.

"It's a lovely, sunny
day," went on Dog.

"And you should be
HAPPY!" finished Cat.

"But I AM happy," Teddy told them.
"It's just that my mouth turns down at the
corners. And I can't do anything about it."

"Good heavens!" cried Cat. SHE had a
smile as wide as her face.

"Do you mean you were MADE that way?"
grinned Dog and Rabbit together.

Teddy nodded sadly. "However happy I
feel inside," he explained, "I always
LOOK miserable. If only I had just a
small smile, then I'm sure Boy would
spend more time with me."

That night, when Teddy was asleep,
Rabbit, Dog and Cat lay awake. At last
they came up with a plan.

Next day they told Teddy what he must do.

"Will it hurt?" he asked.

Rabbit, Dog and Cat shook their heads. "Not much," they said.

After supper Boy had his bath.

"Just look at this tee-shirt!" cried his Mum. "It's almost torn in half."

And, with that, she opened the bathroom door and threw the tee-shirt across the hallway. The tee-shirt landed on the mending pile.

"NOW!" cried Rabbit, Dog and Cat.

Teddy leaned over the edge of the top bunk. "OUCH!" He bounced onto the floor, across the hallway and straight on top of the mending pile.

When Boy woke up next morning, Teddy was propped at the end of his bed. Rabbit, Dog and Cat grinned and waited.

"And what are YOU smiling about?" Boy asked Teddy.

But Teddy didn't say a word. He just smiled back.

"Come on," cried Boy suddenly. He grabbed Teddy and leapt out of bed.

"It's a lovely, sunny day. And we're going to play outside together... ALL MORNING!"

Another story tomorrow.

Teddy and the Talent Show

Teddy and Tom were excited. They were about to watch a Talent Show.

"I do hope there'll be a trick cyclist," said Tom.

"Well, I want to see some real magic," thought Teddy. And he peered out from his tipped-up seat.

The first act was a group of singers. They were very good and Teddy tapped his paw, while Tom hummed to the music.

Next came a comedian. Tom couldn't stop laughing at the jokes. And Teddy nearly fell off his seat.

Then Tom got his wish and a trick cyclist sped onto the stage.

"WOW!" whispered Tom. "I can barely balance on two wheels, let alone one."

"And I still need three and a knee," thought Teddy.

The next act was a troupe of dancers. Teddy and Tom looked at each other, and yawned! But there was still one act to follow.

"Now, last," boomed the voice of the presenter, "but by no means least," he added cheerfully, "I give you... MALCOLM THE MAGICIAN!"

Teddy sat bolt upright. And, when Malcolm asked for a volunteer from the audience, somehow Teddy's arm shot up with all the rest.

Malcolm pretended to take a long time choosing. "The young man in the striped dungarees," he announced at last.

First Teddy was put in a special box.

"OOOOOOH" went the audience. It looked just as if Malcolm was sawing Teddy in two!

Then he made him disappear and reappear with a rabbit.

In fact, Teddy helped Malcolm with all his tricks. And at the end of the act the applause was deafening.

That night Mum asked Tom if he had enjoyed the Show.

"Oh Mum," cried Tom, "it was... MAGIC!"

And Teddy couldn't help but agree.

Another story tomorrow.

My Owner

My owner has a rumply bed;
She sometimes doesn't wash!
But even when she snores or squirms,
I never mind a squash.

"Let's play a game," she sometimes cries,
And "Teddy, you begin,"
But sometimes when we play
  a game,
I WISH she'd let me win.

My owner sometimes stamps and shouts,
(She's not a pretty sight!)
But even when the grown-ups glare,
I'M there to hold her tight.

My owner likes to go on trips,
By boat or train or bus;
And if I didn't go as well,
I know there'd be a fuss.

We have our ups and downs of days,
But still we both agree,
I wouldn't change her for the world,
And nor would she change me.

The end.